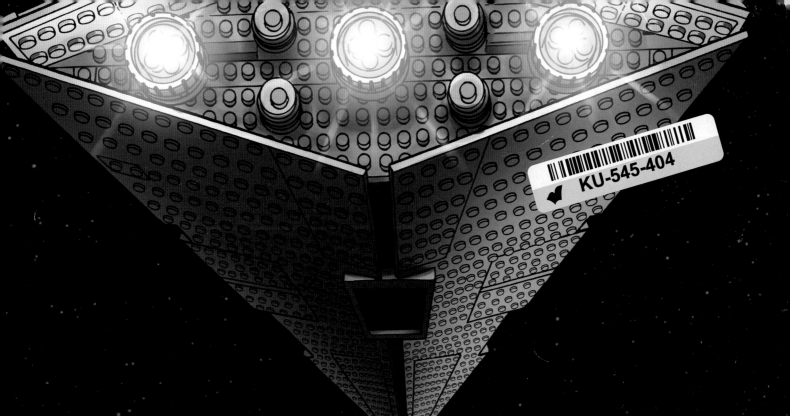

A LONG TIME AGO IN A GALAXY FAR, FAR AWAY. . .

The evil Darth Vader was hunting a brave young princess who had stolen the instructions for the Empire's wickedest weapon the Death Star.

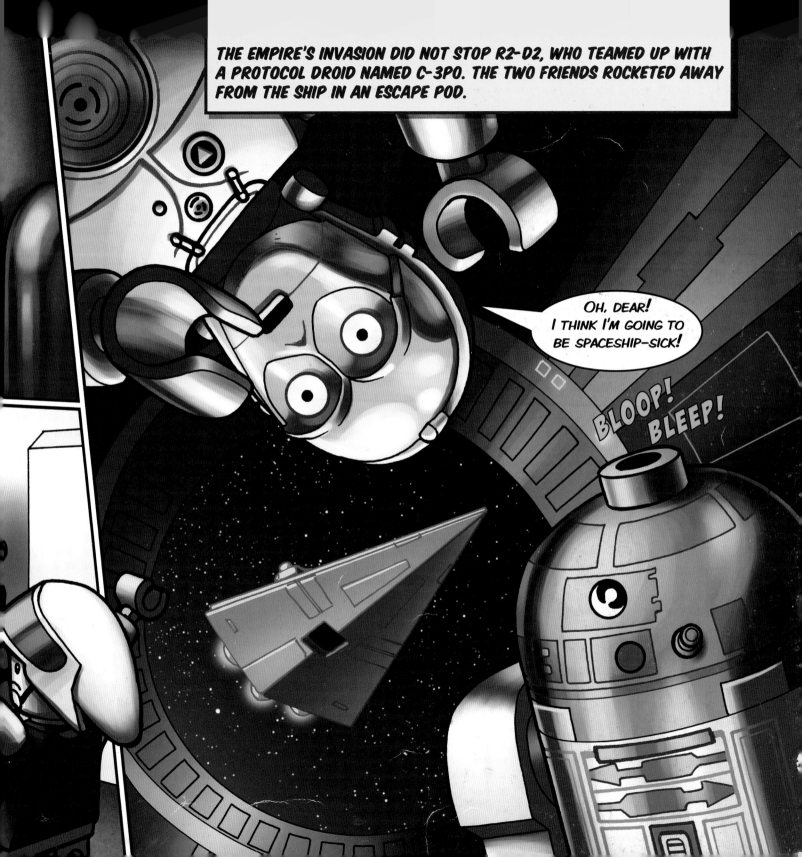

LUCKILY, LUKE AND HIS UNCLE OWEN HAD A VERY SPECIFIC NEED FOR A PROTOCOL DROID. THEY BOUGHT BOTH C-3PO AND R2-D2.

LUKE AND THE DROIDS RUSHED OVER TO KENOBI'S HOUSE. THERE, LUKE LEARNED THAT NOT ONLY WAS BEN KENOBI ONCE A JEDI KNIGHT, BUT THAT LUKE'S FATHER WAS A JEDI, TOO! AND NOW IT WAS UP TO LUKE AND OBI-WAN (BEN) KENOBI TO DESTROY THE DEATH STAR AND STOP THE EMPIRE BEFORE THEY TOOK CONTROL OF THE GALAXY.

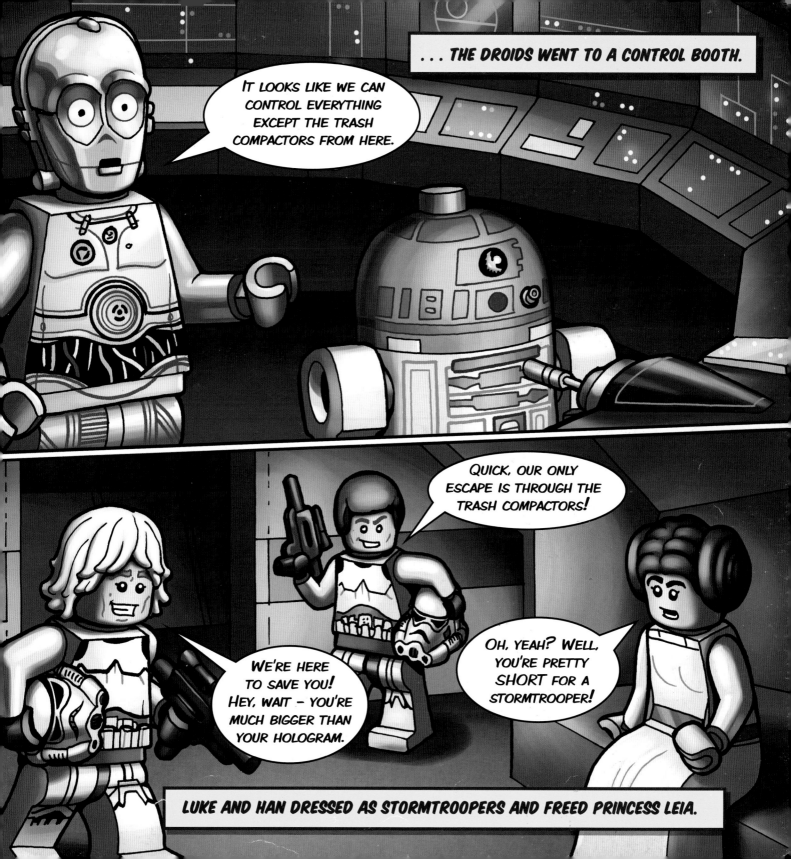

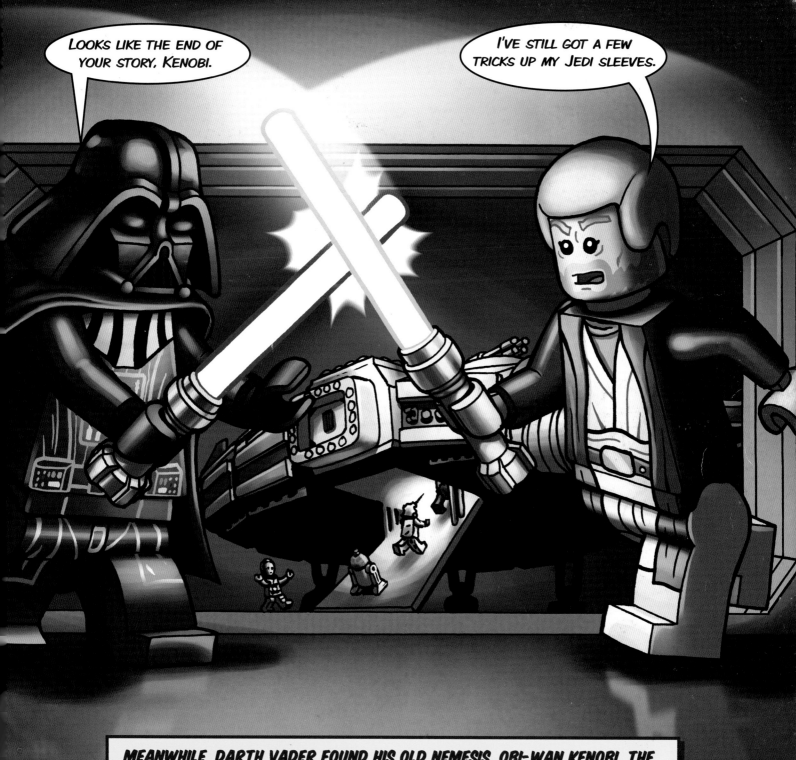

MEANWHILE, DARTH VADER FOUND HIS OLD NEMESIS, OBI-WAN KENOBI. THE SITH LORD AND THE JEDI BATTLED UNTIL KENOBI WAS SURE THAT LUKE, LEIA AND THE CREW HAD SAFELY ESCAPED.

THE X-WINGS STRUCK FIRST, BUT THEY WERE OVERPOWERED BY HUNDREDS OF TIE FIGHTERS. LUKE MANAGED TO DODGE AND WEAVE HIS WAY TOWARDS THE DEATH STAR'S ONE WEAK SPOT.

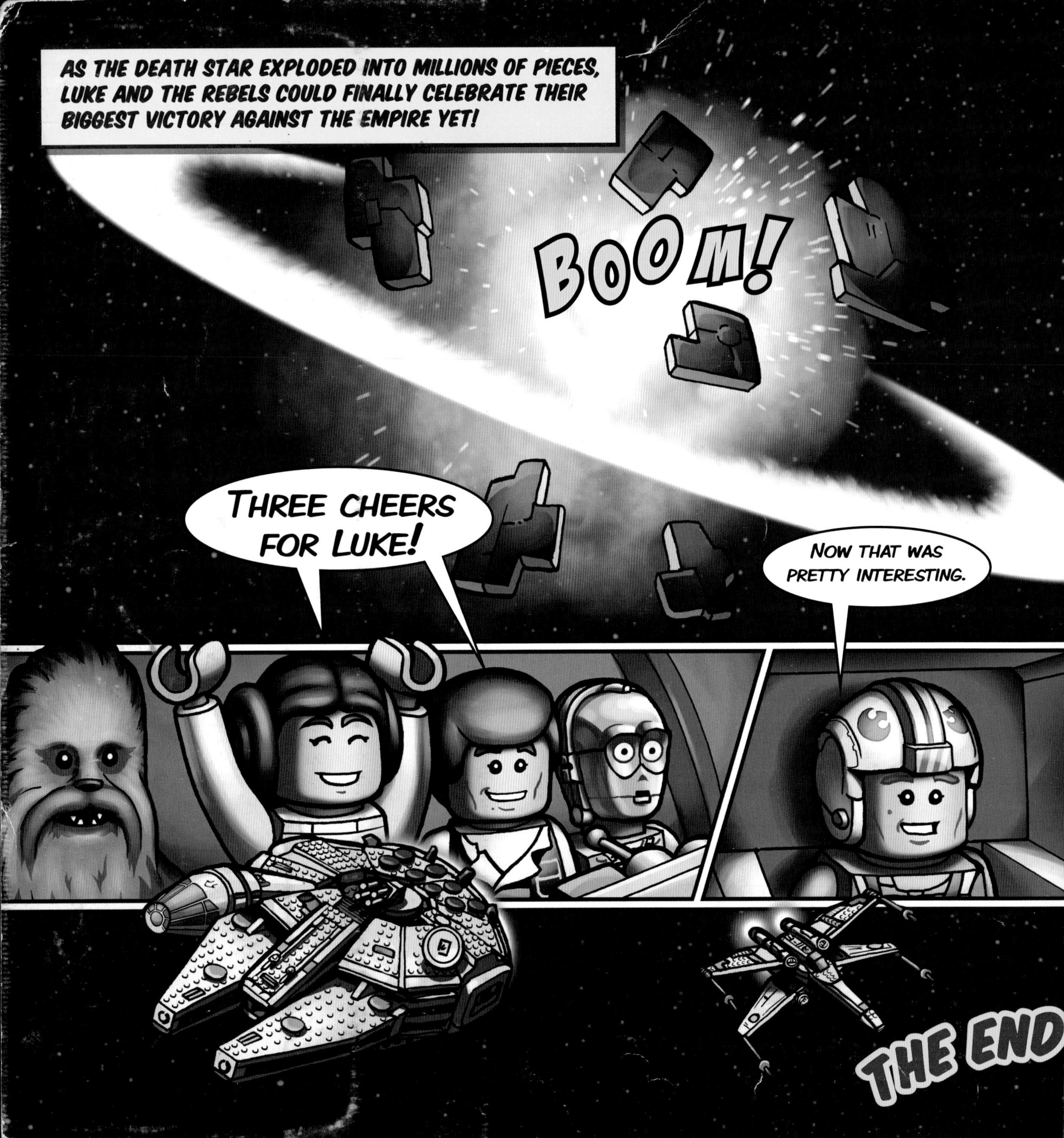
AS THE DEATH STAR EXPLODED INTO MILLIONS OF PIECES, LUKE AND THE REBELS COULD FINALLY CELEBRATE THEIR BIGGEST VICTORY AGAINST THE EMPIRE YET!
BOOM!
THREE CHEERS FOR LUKE!
NOW THAT WAS PRETTY INTERESTING.
THE END